Anna and the Flowers of Winter

Retold by Nettie Lowenstein
Illustrated by Elizabeth Harbour

PUFFIN BOOKS

For my husband, Llewellyn – E. H.

In memory of my husband, Heinz Bernard – N. L.

PUFFIN BOOKS

Published by the Penguin Group
Penguin Books Ltd, 27 Wrights Lane, London W8 5TZ, England
Penguin Putnam Inc., 375 Hudson Street, New York, New York 10014, USA
Penguin Books Australia Ltd, Ringwood, Victoria, Australia
Penguin Books Canada Ltd, 10 Alcorn Avenue, Toronto, Ontario, Canada M4V 3B2
Penguin Books (NZ) Ltd, Private Bag 102902, NSMC, Auckland, New Zealand

Penguin Books Ltd, Registered Offices: Harmondsworth, Middlesex, England

On the World Wide Web at: www.penguin.com

First published by Viking 1999
Published in Puffin Books 2000
1 3 5 7 9 10 8 6 4 2

Text copyright © Nettie Lowenstein, 1999
Illustrations copyright © Elizabeth Harbour, 1999
All rights reserved

The moral right of the author and illustrator has been asserted

Made and printed in Italy by Printer Trento Srl

British Library Cataloguing in Publication Data
A CIP catalogue record for this book is available from the British Library

ISBN 0–140–56554–X

Once, long ago, there was a little girl called Anna. She lived
with her stepmother and her stepsister in a little wooden
house in a village on the edge of a great forest. Anna worked
hard all day long, washing and scrubbing, cooking and cleaning,
fetching wood and water, and doing everything her stepmother
and her stepsister wanted her to do. But they didn't like her.
They didn't like her at all.

One bitterly cold day in winter, when the world outside was
covered in deep snow and ice, Anna's stepsister said
suddenly, "Go into the forest and bring me back some violets."

Anna could hardly believe her ears.

"But it's winter," she said to her sister. "It's December. Violets
don't flower in December. They flower in March."

"You heard your sister," said her stepmother. "Go and get those
violets." And she opened the door of the house and pushed Anna
out without even a coat to keep her warm.

"Don't come back till you've got them," shouted the stepmother.
"We won't let you in."

She closed the door with a great bang.

*P*oor Anna went into the forest not knowing what to do or where to go. How could she find violets in the middle of winter? Yet how could she go home without them?

The forest was still and white and cold. The snow was deep on the ground and the branches of the trees were laden with it.

As Anna wandered she grew colder and colder, until she felt sure she would soon freeze to death.

Then, in the distance, she saw lights – orange and yellow and red lights. What were they, flickering through the trees? She went towards them. They were flames of a fire! She hurried now, longing to feel its warmth.

As she drew nearer, Anna saw a group of men sitting round the fire on low seats. There was one higher, bigger seat, and on it sat a very old man with a huge white beard which looked like sparkling snow and glittering ice.

Anna went up to the very old man on the highest, biggest seat, because he seemed to be the leader, and she said, "Please, may I warm myself by your fire? I'm so very cold."

He smiled at her. "Go through, child," he said. "Go through the circle. Stand by the fire and get warm."

So she went through the circle to the fire. She warmed her front and she warmed her back and, oh, how lovely it was to stop feeling cold.

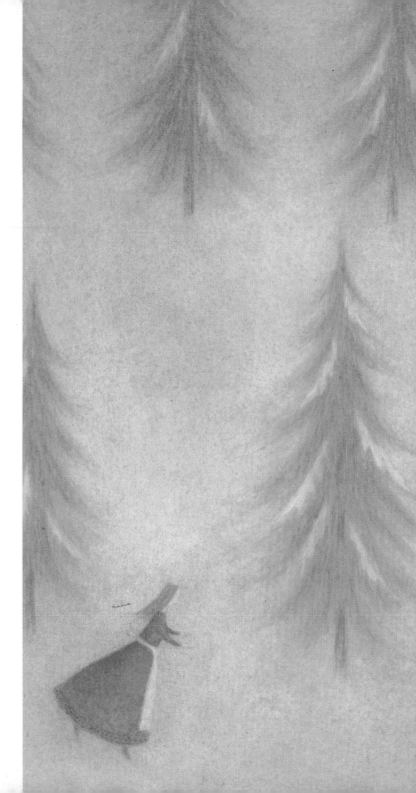

"Why are you wandering alone through the forest", asked the old, old man, "without even a coat to keep you warm? Why are you out in this bitter winter cold?"

"My stepmother and stepsister sent me to pick violets and I had no time to put on my coat."

"You won't find violets in December!" said the old man in amazement. "They don't flower until March."

"I told them that, but they said I mustn't come home without them. I must stay in the forest until I find some."

"It's lucky you met us then," said the old man, and the other men nodded and smiled. "For we are the Twelve Months of the Year, and I am December, the last month, so I am the oldest. I rule now; that's why I sit on the high seat."

Then Anna saw that there were twelve men sitting in the circle. They were all of different ages, starting with the youngest one, on December's left, and getting older and older. They wore splendid clothes made of fur and velvet, green and brown and silver and gold.

December turned to the other Months. "We must help our little friend. March must rule for a short time so that she can have her violets. Do you all agree?"

The eleven Months nodded and one of them said, "We agree."

*A*ll Twelve Months rose from their seats and each one moved three places. Now March was sitting on the high seat.

"Wait," said March to Anna. "Wait and watch."

The cold wind became a warm breeze. The snow began to melt, the ice slipped off the branches of the trees, the birds began to sing. In the distance, Anna saw flowers appearing, hundreds and hundreds of violets.

"Quick!" said March. "Pick your violets! Hurry! Hurry! We can't stay like this for long!"

Anna ran to the clearing, bent down, and gathered as many violets as she could carry in the skirt of her apron. Then she ran back to the circle.

"Thank you," she said to the Twelve Months.

"Hurry home," said March. "Hurry home while the weather is still warm. We shall have to start moving back to our rightful places in a moment."

So Anna hurried through the forest, holding up her apron filled with violets. By the time she reached the door of the cottage, snow was falling heavily. It covered the little girl and the violets in her apron.

Anna went into the cottage and emptied her apron on to the table. The room was filled with the smell of violets.

"You're making the room all wet!" said her stepmother, as the snow melted. "Get a cloth and wipe it up."

"Where ever did you find those violets?" said her stepsister.

Anna told them about the Twelve Months and what had happened, and as her stepmother and stepsister heard the story they became more and more angry.

"You mean to say you could have anything you wanted, and all you asked for was violets?" said her stepmother angrily.

"Stupid girl," said her stepsister. "Who asks for violets when they could ask for anything?"

"But, sister – " began Anna.

"Violets!" repeated her stepmother in a fury. "You could have asked for apples. You could have asked for grapes. People will pay anything in winter for fruit out of season! We could have sold them in the market and made plenty of money. And you asked for violets!"

Anna's stepsister put on her thick coat and wrapped a heavy shawl round her head and shoulders. "I'm going into the forest to find those Twelve Months of the Year! I'm going to ask for something sensible!" She swept the violets off the table angrily.

"Wait for me," said her mother, and she too put on her coat and her shawl. "We shall go together. Two can carry away more than one."

They opened the door of the cottage, and outside the world was still and white with snow.

"Where's the path?" said the stepsister.

"Never mind the path! Look for the fire!" said the stepmother. "If that stupid girl can find the fire and those men, so can we."

So they made their way towards the
forest and began searching for the fire
and the men. The wind had dropped and it was no
longer snowing. But as they wandered through the forest
their feet sank into thick snow and they grew tired and cold.
    Then, in the distance, through the trees, they saw the light of a fire.
        As they hurried towards it they saw twelve men sitting in a circle.

They went up to December on the highest seat of all.

"You saw my daughter," said the stepmother. "She asked for violets, but we want apples, not violets. We want apples, and grapes —"

"And strawberries," said the stepsister. "Don't forget strawberries, Mother."

"I saw no daughter of yours," said December coldly, looking at the stepmother.

"You stupid old man," shouted the stepmother. "Of course she came here. You know she did. You know you gave her violets."

"It's a waste of time talking to him, Mother," said the stepsister. And she turned to January sitting on December's left.

"You look a nice sensible lad," she said. "You heard what we've come for. We want strawberries, apples and grapes."

January smiled. "You'll get what you deserve," he said, and he turned to the rest of the Months. "Do you agree?" he asked them. They all nodded. "Let us move places then," he said.

The twelve men rose from their seats and moved one seat to the right. January was now sitting on the high seat. "Wait and watch," he said. "Wait and watch."

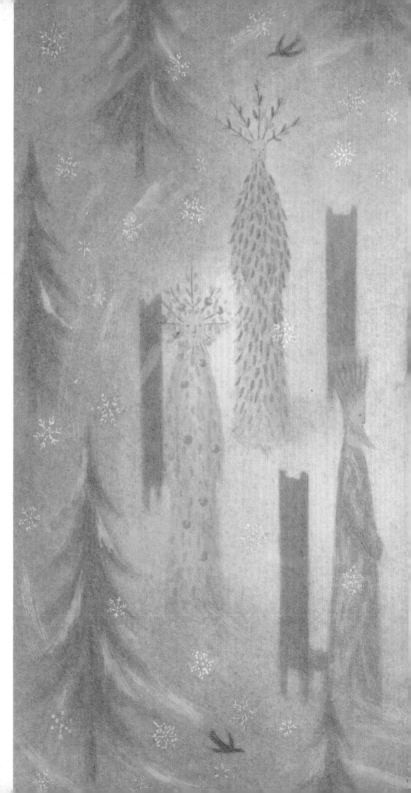

Suddenly the wind blew with an icy blast. The stepmother and stepsister were lifted high into the air and carried far into the forest. And the wind shrieked and the snow fell and the trees shook their heads and dropped great quantities of snow on them. On and on they went, deeper and deeper into the forest. It was as if they were being swallowed up by the storm.

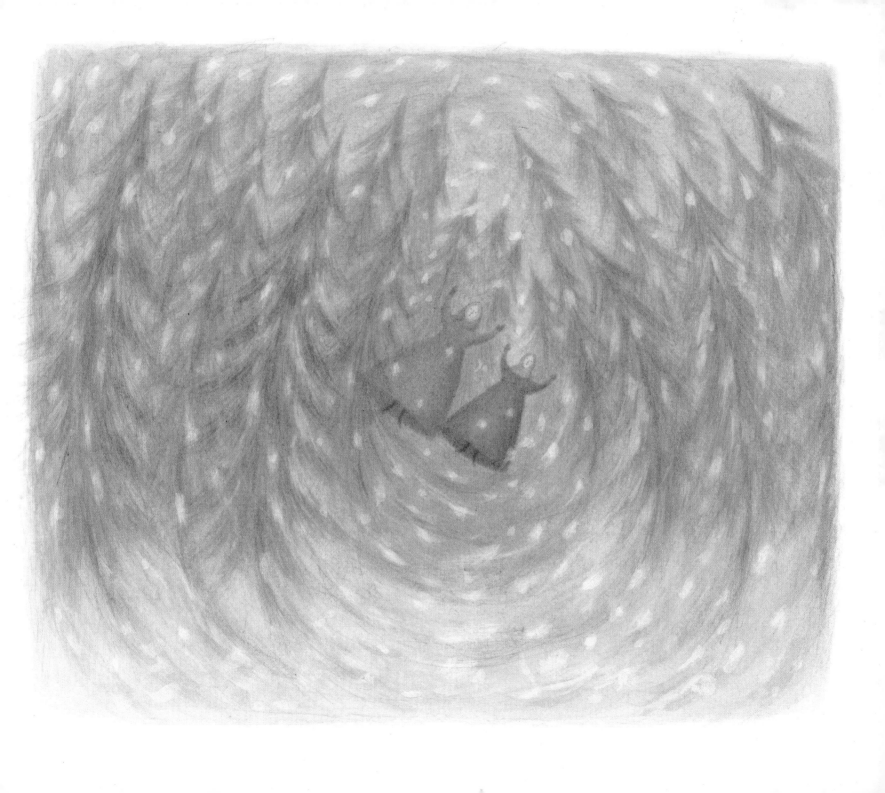

Day after day Anna waited for her stepmother and stepsister to return. At last she knew they would never come home. She did not miss them. She lived very happily in the little wooden house on the edge of the forest. People marvelled at her garden. Everything – flowers, fruit and vegetables – grew there in abundance all the year round.

*B*ut in the heart of the forest, where people rarely wandered, two trees were standing, bare and black and twisted. And always, whenever the wind blew, they scratched against each other and grumbled and complained.